FOX RIVER VALLEY PLD
3 1783 00470 5988

W9-BRO-830

Big Bear's Big Boat

by EVE BUNTING

Illustrated by Nancy Carpenter

CLARION BOOKS
Houghton Mifflin Harcourt
Boston • New York

Clarion Books
215 Park Avenue South
New York, New York 10003

Clarion Books is an imprint of Houghton Mifflin Harcourt Publishing Company.

www.hmhbooks.com

The text of this book was set in 18-point Elysium Book.
The illustrations were executed in pen and ink and digital media.

Library of Congress Cataloging-in-Publication Data
Bunting, Eve, 1928–
Big Bear's big boat / by Eve Bunting ; Illustrated by Nancy Carpenter.
p. cm.
Summary: When Big Bear outgrows his old boat, he gives it to Little Bear and builds himself a new one—just like it except bigger—until his friends start making suggestions that result in something very different.
ISBN 978-0-618-58537-3 (hardcover)
[1. Boats and boating—Fiction. 2. Bears—Fiction.] I. Carpenter, Nancy, ill. II. Title.
PZ7.B91527Bhm 2013
[E]—dc23
2012003974

Manufactured in China
SCP 10 9 8 7 6 5 4 3 2 1
4500418594

TO SLOAN, MY SAILOR SON —E.B.

FOR TANYA —N.C.

When Big Bear grew too big for his little boat, he gave it to Little Bear. Now he was building a big boat for himself.

"I want it to be *just like* my little boat, but bigger," Big Bear told his mother.

His mother smiled. "You loved your little boat, and now Little Bear loves it. You will love your new one just as much."

"I hope so," Big Bear said.

He worked hard, and soon his big boat was finished.

"You are just what I dreamed you would be," he told it fondly.

Big Bear was ready to slide his big boat into Huckleberry Lake when Beaver came by.

"That's a very fine boat," he said. "But a big boat like that needs a mast."

"Maybe you're right," Big Bear said.

So he made a mast for his big boat.

Otter popped his head out of the water. "A fine big boat like that needs a top deck," he said. "All big boats have a top deck so you can sit high up and watch the sun set into the lake and the moon rise over it."

"Maybe you're right," Big Bear said.

So he made a top deck and put it on his big boat.
Blue Heron flew down from the sky.
"What a fine big boat," he said. "But you need a cabin to sleep in. All big boats have a cabin."
"Maybe you're right," Big Bear said.

So he made a cabin and perched it on his big boat.

Then he stepped back and looked. "Oh," he said. "What an ugly big boat I've made. The mast leans over, the deck slants, and the cabin is higgledy-piggledy."

Big Bear knew what was wrong. But he didn't want to hurt his friends' feelings. He thought hard.

"All of you tried to help me," he said. "And I thank you. But I'm still the same bear I was before. Only now I'm bigger. And this boat is not my dream. A bear should never let go of his own dream."

"Maybe you're right," Beaver said.

Otter nodded. "I think you are."

Blue Heron craned his long neck. "There's no doubt about it."

So Big Bear took down the mast that leaned over, removed the higgledy-piggledy cabin, took off the deck that slanted . . .

and smiled at his big boat.

Then he slid it into Huckleberry Lake and rowed all around.

He fished from it.

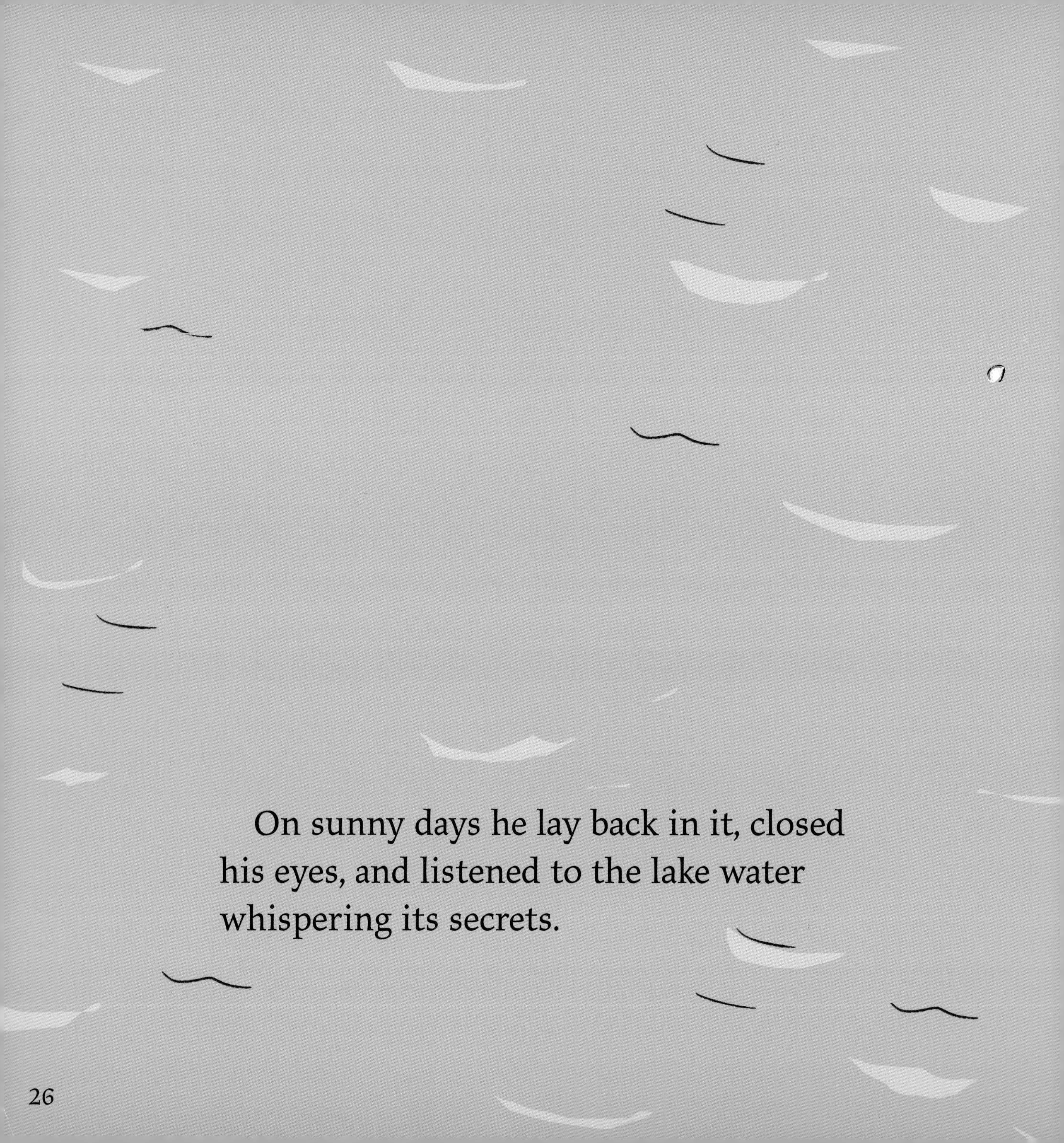

On sunny days he lay back in it, closed his eyes, and listened to the lake water whispering its secrets.

At night he watched the sun set into the lake and the moon rise over it.

Sometimes there was a shooting star.

When he saw Little Bear in his little boat on Huckleberry Lake, Big Bear waved, and Little Bear waved back.

How nice it is to be us, Big Bear thought. *Two brown bears in two fine boats sailing on a blue, blue lake.*

And he was happy.